The Best Nickname

By Dina Anastasio
Illustrated by Tom Garcia

A GOLDEN BOOK • NEW YORK
Western Publishing Company, Inc., Racine, Wisconsin 53404

Nicky needed a nickname.

All the other members of the Sixth Street Club had a nickname.

Sam had a nickname.

Everyone in the club called him "Second Base Sam," because Sam could slide into second base better than anyone else in Fredericksburg.

David had a nickname.

Everyone called him "The Drummer," because David could play the drums better than anyone else in second grade.

Terry had a nickname.
Everyone called her "Toe Shoes Terry," because Terry was such a great dancer.

Lucy had a nickname.
Everyone called her "The Runner," because Lucy could run faster than anyone else in the Sixth Street Club.

But Nicky didn't have a nickname.

He couldn't play baseball very well, and he couldn't play the drums. He couldn't dance, and he'd never won a race in his life.

Everyone in the club just called him Nicky.

Nicky thought about nicknames all the time. He thought
about them when he was fixing up the clubhouse...

...and when he was helping his mother do the dishes...

...and when he was helping his little sister do her arithmetic.

One time, when Nicky was playing street hockey, he thought, "Maybe I could call myself 'The Hockey Player.'"

But then he fell down. "Hmm," thought Nicky. "Maybe that's not such a good name after all."

Another time, when Nicky was building a fort at the beach, he thought, "Maybe I could call myself 'The Architect.' "

But when the tunnel in his fort caved in, he decided that that wasn't a good name either.

On the morning of The Drummer's birthday, Nicky woke up very early. He got out his paper and paints and started making a sign.

When he was almost finished, he held it up and said, "Gee, this is pretty good. Maybe I could call myself 'The Artist.'"

HAPPY BIRTHDAY
TO THE
DRUMMER

Nicky liked the sound of that name. He smiled and went back to work. Suddenly, he knocked over his jar of red paint.

"Darn!" Nicky said. "A real artist wouldn't do that. I guess I can't call myself 'The Artist.'"

Nicky threw the sign away and started all over again.

When Nicky was finished with his sign, he went
downtown and bought a cake and some balloons. On the
way back, he saw Second Base Sam. He was practicing his
swing.

"Whatcha got?" asked Second Base Sam.

Nicky showed him the sign.

"Wow," said Second Base Sam. "That's a really nice thing to do. The Drummer will love it."

Nicky and Second Base Sam walked down Maple Street until they came to Toe Shoes Terry's house. She was doing pirouettes.

When Toe Shoes Terry saw Nicky's sign, she said, "Oh, no! I forgot all about The Drummer's birthday! It's a good thing you remembered, Nicky. You always remember things like that."

HAPPY BIRTHDAY
TO THE
DRUMMER

Just then The Runner ran by. "Race you to the clubhouse," she said.

"Not me," said Nicky. "I don't want to ruin The Drummer's cake."

So the others took off down Sixth Street. They ran through The Drummer's yard to the clubhouse. The Runner touched it first, just as she always did.

When Nicky arrived, Toe Shoes Terry took the sign and held it up.

"Look what Nicky made," she told The Runner.

"That's swell," The Runner said. "You always do such nice things, Nicky. I remember the time you baked cupcakes for us, and the time you made up the club password. I'll bet you're the only one who remembered The Drummer's birthday."

Everyone followed Nicky into the clubhouse. He hung up his sign while the others blew up the balloons.

Nicky was putting the cake on the table when he heard a familiar sound—*Boom, ba ba boom, ba ba boom.*

"It's The Drummer!" said Second Base Sam.

HAPPY BIRTHDAY TO THE DRUMMER

The Drummer came into the clubhouse and looked at the sign. Then he said to Nicky, "You made this, didn't you?"

Nicky nodded.

"I knew it," said The Drummer.

The Sixth Street Club sat around the table and shared the birthday cake. When they were finished eating, Nicky said, "I made up a song for The Drummer, but it's kind of silly."

"Sing it, Nicky," said Toe Shoes Terry.

"Well, okay," said Nicky. "But don't laugh."

Nicky stood up and started to sing:

"Happy Birthday to The Drummer,
Happy Birthday to The Drummer,
We're all here to show you,
We're glad that we know you.

"Whenever you come here,
When you come with your drum here,
Well I guess this sounds sappy,
But you make us feel happy!"

When Nicky was finished, his friends clapped and cheered.

"You're the greatest!" shouted Second Base Sam.

Toe Shoes Terry started to whistle. "Nicky, you're the nicest!" she said.

"You're terrific!" said The Runner.

"No," said The Drummer, banging on his drum. "You're the best!"

"The best!" the friends all shouted together.
"The best?" said Nicky.
"The best!"
And from that day on, Nicky had a nickname. Everyone called him "The Best," because that's just what he was.